Postman Pat™

092

£4.50

This book belongs to

name ....

address ....

....

.... postcode ....

Stories and features written by Brenda Apsley and illustrated by Ray Mutimer and Edgar Hodges

Copyright © Woodland Animations Ltd, 1991

Published in Great Britain by World International Publishing Limited, an Egmont Company, Egmont House, PO Box 111, Great Ducie Street, Manchester M60 3BL.

Printed in Italy

ISBN 0 7498 0270 7

Contents

Julian's photograph album

Postman Pat's son, Julian, was given a camera for his last birthday. He tried it out by taking photographs of his friends and neighbours in Greendale. He stuck the photographs in an album and wrote everyone's names under their pictures. How many of the people do you know?

Doctor Gilbertson

Mum and Dad

Reverend Timms

Colonel Forbes

MRS Goggins

PC Selby

Ted Glen

Miss Hubbard

MR & Mrs Thompson

Peter Fogg

George Lancaster

Sam Waldron

Mrs Pottage

Granny Dryden

7

Tom and Katy and baby Paul

Charlie Pringle

Sarah Gilbertson

Lucy Selby

Bill Thompson

me

Fancy dress

"Are you coming to the fancy dress contest on Friday, Pat?" asked Miss Hubbard one morning. "The whole village is going to be there – and I've organized a wonderful prize for the best outfit."

"Oh, yes," said Pat. "I like fancy dress. I'll be there."

Miss Hubbard waved as she cycled away. "Village hall, seven o'clock. See you there!"

The rest of the week was a busy one for the people of Greendale. They were all going to the fancy dress party, and they all wanted to win the prize for the best outfit. They kept their ideas secret.

At Forge Cottage, Pat, Sara and Julian made their own outfits.

Julian found Sara rummaging in her sewing box. "I need some gold buttons for my outfit," she said.

"Why, what are you going as?" asked Julian.

"Never you mind," said Sara. "It's a secret."

Gold buttons, thought Julian. I bet Mum's going as a soldier.

Julian asked Sara if she had any blue fabric he could use. She found some for him. I bet he's going to dress up as a sailor, she thought.

Pat collected things for his costume in the garden shed. He had a dustbin lid, a kitchen colander – and two bananas! What on earth was Pat going to dress up as?

Everyone else in Greendale was busy, too, sewing, glueing and cutting.

"Can I borrow a black tie, Pat?" asked Peter Fogg.

Aha, thought Pat. I bet Peter's dressing up as a schoolboy. He'll probably turn up wearing short trousers!

Dorothy Thompson went to Ted Glen's workshop. "Have you got a bit of wire I could have?" she asked. "It's for my outfit."

Ted gave Dorothy some wire. "You're the third person today to ask me for wire," he said. He was puzzled – what could they be planning to dress up as?

Sarah Gilbertson saw her mum painting an old pair of boots with shiny black paint. Mum must be dressing up as a policeman, she thought.

Julia Pottage went to Mrs Goggins' house. "Have you any scraps of orange wool I could use for the fancy dress contest on Friday?" asked Julia.

Mrs Goggins found some wool in her work basket and handed it to Julia. "Are you going as a . . ." Mrs Goggins started to ask, but Julia rushed out of the door.

"It's a secret. Wait and see," said Julia. "Goodbye – and thanks for the wool."

On Friday Pat had a lot of post to deliver. It was late afternoon when he made his last call and turned back towards Greendale. He glanced down at Jess, who was sitting beside him. "It's been a long day today, but I've just got time to go home for tea, then put my fancy dress outfit on. It's very good, if I do say so myself. I think I might just win that first prize."

HIIIISSSSSSSS!

"What's that?" said Pat.

Clouds of white steam started to billow out of the van's engine. "Oh, no," said Pat, putting his foot on the brake.

Pat looked in the engine, which was full of hot, swirling, hissing steam. There was nothing he could do. He sat on the side of the road and waited. Jess sat beside him. "We'll wait for someone to come along," said Pat. "Then I can ring for help."

Pat and Jess waited . . .

and waited . . .

and waited . . .

But no one came. It was a quiet lane, and there was no traffic. Everyone will be on their way to the village hall now, thought Pat sadly.

Pat was just about to start walking home when he saw a bike coming along the lane. It was PC Selby. Pat waved at him, and he stopped.

Pat explained what had happened.

"I can't give you and Jess a lift on my bike," said PC Selby. "But I'll send the breakdown truck."

It was half past seven when Pat and Jess got to Greendale. It was too late to go home for his outfit, but Pat decided to go to the village hall anyway, to see the others.

What a shock Pat got when he opened the door! There in the village hall were lots and lots of Postman Pats, in all shapes and sizes. Everyone had had the same idea for their fancy dress outfit – even Sara and Julian!

"Is that you, Pat?" said the Reverend Timms. "Come in. I'm having terrible trouble judging the contest. How can I decide whose outfit is best?"

Reverend Timms looked around the hall. Mrs Goggins, Julia Pottage, Doctor Gilbertson, Peter Fogg, Sam Waldron – even Colonel Forbes – were all dressed as Postman Pat.

Then Reverend Timms smiled. He walked to the stage. "It has been difficult to decide who should get first prize," he said. "But I think there can only be one winner – Pat Clifton. He is the original Postman Pat, after all!"

Did you guess what Pat was going to dress up as? The dustbin lid was a shield, and Pat had tied the two bananas to the colander and planned to wear it as a helmet. Yes, Pat was dressing up as a Viking!

Pick out Postman Pat

Can you find the real Postman Pat in the village hall?
Look carefully – he's in there somewhere!

Pat and Jess have stopped for a cup of tea at Granny Dryden's.

Granny is doing some knitting. Jess likes the look of her wool!

Jess starts playing with Granny Dryden's wool. It's great fun!

But he soon runs out of wool. It has unravelled on the floor.

Pat is ready to go now. "Thanks for the tea," he tells Granny.

But Pat can't move his feet . . . Jess has tied them up with wool!

Fruit salad

It was Postman Pat's day off. He looked out of the window. It was a crisp spring day. "Right," he said, and put on some old clothes – a sweater with holes in it, paint-spattered trousers, wellington boots and an old tweed hat.

Pat sat at the breakfast table. "I'm going to spend all day in the garden," he said.

"As a scarecrow?" asked Julian, laughing.

Pat looked at his old clothes and smiled. "Cheek!" he said. "No, I'm going to plant some new fruit bushes and vegetable seeds."

"Oh good," said Sara. "Lovely fresh fruit and vegetables."

Pat bought fruit bushes and packets of vegetable seeds at the garden centre, and laid them on the grass.

He dug over the soil using a big spade, then dug a hole for each fruit bush. He planted the bushes in rows and watered them.

Sara came out with a mug of coffee. "How's it going?" she asked.

"Fine," said Pat. "But I could do without this wind. It keeps blowing my hat off."

WHOOSH!

A gust of wind blew into the garden and lifted Pat's hat off his head. "There it goes again," said Pat, bending down to pick up the hat.

"Don't forget to put labels on the bushes, will you?" said Sara.

"I'll tie them on later," said Pat. "Look, I've put the label in front of each bush."

Next Pat hoed the soil in the vegetable patch. He made lines with the side of the hoe and sprinkled in seeds. There were lots – cabbages, cauliflowers, peas, beans, carrots and lettuces. He covered the seeds with soil. "Now I'll put the empty seed packets on sticks in front of each row so we'll know what's planted where," he said.

Pat bent down to pick up the empty seed packets he had laid in front of each row – but a big gust of wind swept into the garden and swirled them up into the air. Pat held on to his hat and watched as the seed packets and labels rushed around. It looked like a little whirlwind.

When the wind dropped, the labels and seed packets floated down to the ground. But they were all mixed up, of course. "Oh, no," said Pat, picking up the packets and labels. He looked at a seed packet with a picture of cabbages on the front. "Now did I put the cabbages in the first row – or the third?" he said to himself. "And is this a gooseberry or a redcurrant bush?" It was hard to tell – the bare bushes all looked alike.

Pat went into the kitchen and put the labels and seed packets in a big heap on the table. "Look," said Pat. "I was just going to tie on the labels and put the seed packets on sticks when a big gust of wind mixed them all up."

"Oh dear," said Sara. "How will we know what's growing where?"

"That's a good question," said Pat, taking off his old tweed hat and scratching his head.

Suddenly Pat smiled. "I've got it!" he said, and before Sara could speak Pat had rushed out into the garden again.

Pat disappeared into the shed and Sara heard banging. What was Pat doing?

Pat came out of the shed carrying two wooden stakes with labels on top. He knocked them into the ground, one in front of the fruit bushes, one in front of the vegetable patch.

Then he stepped out of the way so that Sara could read the labels.

One said FRUIT SALAD; and the other said MIXED VEGETABLES.

Sara laughed. "That's a good idea – for a scarecrow!" she said.

Which flower?

There are lots of birds and insects in Pat's garden. Who flies to each flower? Follow the trails to find out.

Hair today, green tomorrow!

Sam Waldron was selling a special kind of shampoo in the back of his van. "It's for grey hair," he said.

"I would like some, to get rid of my grey hairs," said Pat. "I think they make me look far too old!"

"Nonsense, Pat," Granny Dryden laughed. "I have the most grey hair." She bought two bottles.

Colonel Forbes did not like his grey hair. "I look one hundred years old with all this grey hair," he sighed.

Almost everyone in the village bought some of Sam's special shampoo for covering grey hair.

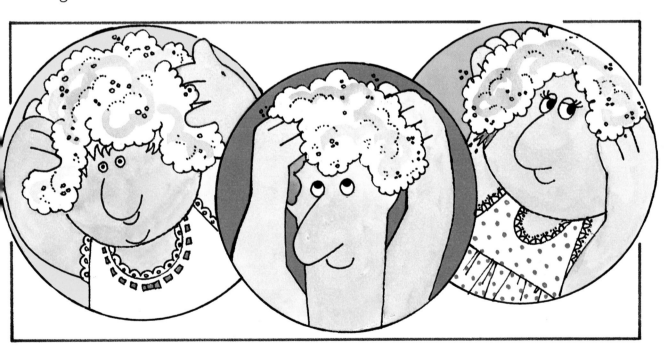

That evening, everyone who bought the shampoo washed their hair with it. It smelled rather nice.

"Hmm!" said Pat. "It has a strong smell, but I like it. I wonder what my hair will look like tomorrow?"

In the morning, Pat could not believe his eyes. His hair was bright green. He went out to find Sam.

Pat bumped into others looking for Sam. "My poor hair!" cried Granny Dryden. "Where is Sam?"

They found Sam looking at the shampoo. "I made a mistake," Sam said. "It is *green* shampoo, not grey!"

They all had to laugh. "It will wash out," he said. "Anyway, you all look trendy now."

Mooooooo . . .

It was a lovely summer's day. The sun was shining and the birds were singing. "Just the day for a walk in the country," said Postman Pat as he, Sara and Julian ate breakfast.

"But Charlie's coming round to play today," said Julian.

"No problem," said Pat. "He can come with us. I'll ring his mum and tell her he'll be with us all day."

Soon after breakfast, Pat, Sara, Julian and Charlie set off.

They walked all morning. Then Julian said, "I'm hungry. And thirsty."

Pat looked at his watch. "No problem. It's nearly lunchtime." He patted the large picnic basket he was carrying. "And here's our lunch."

Sara looked around. "Look, there's the perfect spot for a picnic," she said. "Just in front of that hedge. The ground's nice and flat and the hedge will make a good windbreak."

Pat and Sara unpacked the picnic. There were bread rolls, hard boiled eggs, cold sausages, fruit and yogurt. And a flask of cold orange juice to drink.

21

When Julian and Charlie couldn't eat any more, Julian looked around.

"I'm bored," he said. "Can we go now?"

Pat and Sara were lying down, eyes closed. "No, we're having a rest before we set off again," said Pat. "Why don't you run around for a bit? Play tag?"

"It's too hot," said Julian.

"How about a game of I-Spy?" said Pat. "You always enjoy that."

"Yes!" said Charlie and Julian together.

They spied grass, sun, clouds, birds. Then Julian nudged Pat's arm. "Dad, Dad," he said.

"What? Where? Who?" said Pat, sitting up quickly and looking around. He'd been daydreaming, and had almost fallen asleep.

"It's only me, Dad," said Julian. "Can we go now? We've played I-Spy, but there aren't enough things to spy out here."

"Your mum and I want to stay here for a while. We're enjoying the sun," said Pat. "Aren't we, Sara?"

"Mmmm," said Sara. She opened her eyes. "I know a good game. We take it in turns to make an animal noise. The others have to guess what animal we're supposed to be."

"Great," said Pat. "And we'll join in, so there's more variety. We can play lying down. All right?"

"Yes," said Julian. "I'll go first.

"Eeek! Eeek!" said Julian. "Eeek! Eeek!"

"Is it a pig?" asked Charlie.

Julian shook his head. "No." He made the noise again. "Eeek! Eeek!"

"I know," said Sara. "It's a mouse, isn't it?"

"Yes," said Julian. "Your turn now, Mum."

Sara said, "Quack, quack, quack."

"That's easy," said Charlie. "It's a duck, right?"

Sara nodded. "Your turn."

Charlie thought hard. "Eee-aw, eee-aw," he said.

"Got it," said Pat before anyone else could speak. "A donkey! Now it's my turn.

"I'm going to think up a hard one," said Pat. "Here it is." Pat made a sort of trumpeting noise. It was loud.

Sara laughed. "Sounds like a one-legged thingymajig to me."

Julian and Charlie looked at each other. What could it be?

"Have you made it up, Mr Clifton?" asked Charlie.

"No," said Pat, and he made the trumpeting noise again. But this time he waved his hand and arm in front of his nose.

Julian saw him. "I know what it is," he said. "An elephant!"

"That's right," said Pat. "Your turn again, Julian."

"I'm going to think of a really good noise now," said Julian.

MOOOOOOO!

"That's not very difficult," said Pat.

"But I didn't say anything," said Julian.

MOOOOOOO!

"Yes you did," said Sara. "And it's very lifelike. You're good at this."

"But I didn't say anything, Mum," said Julian. "Honest."

MOOOOOOO!

Pat opened one eye. The noise was very close to his left ear. He looked at Julian.

MOOOOOOO!

"Funny," said Pat, sitting up. "If it's not you making that noise, then what . . ."

Pat looked to his left and gasped. Poking its huge head through the hedge was a bull! A very angry-looking bull!

MOOOOOOO!

Pat pointed. "Look," he said. "A bull! And it doesn't look very friendly. Come on, I've heard enough animal noises for one day."

Pat and Sara scrambled to their feet and threw plates and cups into the picnic basket. Then all four ran off down the track.

The bull watched them.

MOOOOOOO!

MOOOOOOO!

Why not play the animal noises game with your friends? It's good fun.

Bulls in a field

There are seven bulls in the field. The farmer wants to fence them off from each other, so that each has his own section of field. But he only has three pieces of fencing. Can you show the farmer how to separate the bulls? The pieces of fence can criss-cross each other.

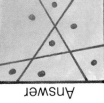

Spaceman Pat

"We are doing well with our rounds today, Jess," says Pat. "I think I've got time for a short break, don't you?"

"I'm enjoying this book," says Pat, picking up a book. "It's an exciting story about a **spaceman**." Jess wants to look!

"I wonder if they have postmen in space?" chuckles Pat. "I suppose people still send letters out there."

"Imagine if **we** had to deliver letters in space," Pat says to Jess. "We'd need special space suits . . ."

Pat starts to daydream about delivering letters to Granny Dryden on the **moon**! "I'm off to **Mars** next," he tells her.

"Be careful, Pat!" calls Granny, as he takes off in his special **post spaceship**. "It's a long way to Mars, you know!"

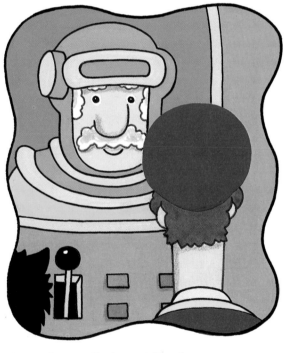

"It doesn't matter how far it is, does it, Jess?" says Pat. "The **space post** must get through, whatever happens!"

Just then, Colonel Forbes appears on Pat's screen. "I'm on my way to see you on Mars," Pat tells him.

"Watch out, then!" warns the Colonel. "There are some nasty **aliens** about." **CRACKLE!** The picture vanishes!

"Oh, no!" groans Pat. "We're under attack! It must be the aliens Colonel Forbes was trying to warn us about!"

"D-don't worry, Jess!" gasps Pat. "I'll protect you! The only thing is . . . who's going to protect **me?** Help . . ."

"**Oh!**" says Pat, waking up suddenly. "Thank goodness for that! It was only a silly daydream. **Phew!**"

Then Pat realizes he can still hear the strange **PARP! PARP! PARP!** noise. It's Reverend Timms honking his car horn!

"Would you move your van, Pat?" asks the Reverend. "I need to get past." "Sorry," says Pat. "I'm on my way now!"

Pat starts the van and moves it out of the way. "I'm off to Colonel Forbes' house now," he tells Reverend Timms.

"I hope the aliens don't get me!" adds Pat, as he drives off. "**Aliens?**" repeats the Reverend, very confused.

Guessing game

It was Christmas time, and the children of Greendale were enjoying their party in the village hall.

They'd played musical chairs and had watched some magic tricks. "And now," said Reverend Timms, "it's time for Charades."

"Charades? What's that?" asked Charles Pringle.

"It's great," said Julian. "It's a sort of guessing game. The person whose turn it is picks out a piece of paper with a title written on it."

"What sort of title?" asked Charlie.

"It could be a book, a play, a film, a song – or a TV programme," said Julian. "Then you have to mime the title. No talking allowed. The others have to guess what it is."

"I see – I think," said Charlie doubtfully.

It was Lucy Selby's turn first. She looked at the piece of paper she'd chosen and made signs for a TV programme with two words. Lucy mimed the second word, making a tall, rounded shape with her hands.

"Mountain?" said Julian.

"Hill?" said Charlie.

Lucy nodded.

"I know," said Sarah Gilbertson. "It's Grange Hill!"

Lucy sat down again. "That's right. Your turn now, Sarah."

Sarah made signs for a book and film with two words. She mimed the second word. She drew a circle with her left hand, and stirred with her right.

"Bowl?" said Charlie.

"Cauldron?" said Bill.

"Pot?" said Katy Pottage.

"Pan?" said Julian.

Sarah nodded, and was about to mime the first word when Julian shouted, "Peter Pan!"

Now it was Julian's turn. He made signs for a book title with two words and thought for a second.

Julian started to wriggle and twitch.

"Snake?" said Charlie.

"Worm?" said Tom Pottage.

Julian twisted and turned. He reached his left arm over his shoulder and pulled an awful face.

"Monster?" said Katy.

"King Kong?" said Charlie.

"Quasimodo?" said Bill.

Julian wriggled and writhed. He reached his right hand up his back and squirmed around.

"A gorilla?" said Tom.

"Beauty and the Beast?" said Sarah.

Julian shouted out, "There's a feather down my back!"

Everyone laughed. "You're not supposed to speak, you know," said Lucy.

Julian put his hand up his sweater and pulled out a long, tickly feather. He sat down.

"That was good," Charlie whispered. "But I've never heard of a book called 'There's a feather down my back'. Is it good?"

Julian just groaned.

Peas in a pod

Tom and Katy Pottage are twins. They look exactly alike. Granny Dryden says they're like two peas in a pod. Can you find them in the audience at the school play? Here's a clue: they are **not** sitting together.

Sara has found some muddy footprints. Someone's in trouble!

They're not Pat's. He has two very clean feet!

Julian had his muddy football boots on, but he has taken them off.

And Sara is wearing her slippers, so they're not her footprints.

It looks like the only one with muddy feet today is Jess!

This might be a very good time to go outside for a while!

Pat helps out

Julian rushed in from school one afternoon. "The circus is coming to Pencaster," he said. "Can we go?"

Pat looked up from his paper. "Well, I . . ."

"Oh, please, Dad, can we? I love the circus."

"Just a . . ." said Pat.

"Oh, please, Dad, PLEASE."

Pat took three tickets from his pocket and waved them in front of Julian. "Look, let me get a word in, will you? I got tickets today. Saturday, three o'clock."

"Oh, brilliant, Dad," said Julian. "Thanks, Dad."

The circus was even better than Julian thought it would be.

After the show Julian and Sara joined the queue for a ride on the big dipper. "Coming on, Dad?" asked Julian.

"No, I'll take a stroll around," said Pat. "See you later."

As Pat passed a big tent, a man came out of a slit in the canvas. He was wearing big silvery trousers and shoes with turned up toes. He grabbed Pat's arm. "Here, mate, hold this will you? Back in a minute."

"No, but I, er, just . . ." said Pat – but the man disappeared into the crowd and Pat was left holding the end of a very fat rope.

Pat waited and waited.

Ted Glen came along. "Hello, Pat, what are you doing?" he asked.

Pat held up the rope. "Just holding this for one of the circus people."

"What's on the end of it?" asked Ted.

Pat shrugged. "Don't know."

Julia Pottage and the twins saw Pat. "What's that you've got hold of?" asked Julia.

Pat shrugged again. "I don't know."

Pat waited and waited and waited and waited.

"There you are, Dad," said Julian. "We've looked everywhere for you. Where have you been?" he asked.

"Here. Holding this rope," said Pat. "And before you ask – no, I don't know what's on the end of it."

Julian popped his head through a slit in the canvas tent. "Crikey!" he said, and popped his head out again. "Look, Dad, look!"

Holding the rope

Postman Pat got a real surprise when he found out what was on the end of the rope. Here are some more people, more ropes – and more animals. Untangle the ropes and then answer the questions.

Which animal is Ted Glen holding?
Who is holding the llama?
Who is holding the pony?
Is Julian holding the baby elephant or the lion cub?

Design a stamp

Mrs Goggins sells lots of stamps in the post office. Some are very colourful. Why not design some stamps? Make some for special occasions like Christmas and Bonfire Night – you can even draw your own face on the stamps!

Pirate Pat

It was Pat's day off, and he was enjoying the sunshine in his garden hammock.

The sun was hot, bees buzzed by, birds sang, and the gentle sway of the hammock made Pat feel a little sleepy.

Pat daydreamed and dozed, and began to snore quietly.

"Ahoy!" roared Pirate Pat. "There's the Black Bucket. Come on, me hearties, after her! There's treasure a-plenty aboard that there ship – and it's ours for the taking. Come on, lads!"

Pirate Pat's ship, the Flying Postman, sailed swiftly through the water and soon caught up with the Black Bucket. Pirate Pat called the cabin boy up on deck. "Here, Julian," he said, "take the wheel. We've got work to do!"

With that Pirate Pat and his men – Terrible Ted, Sneaky Sam and Awful Alf – leapt on board the Black Bucket. There was a terrible fight. Swords clashed, fists flew, until the Black Bucket's captain cried, "Enough! Here, take the gold and jewels. We're no match for Pirate Pat and his crew."

"Ha-harrrrgh," laughed Pirate Pat. "The scourge of the seven seas, that's us. Come on, lads, pick up that treasure chest and let's see what else we can plunder."

Back on the Flying Postman, Pirate Pat's parrot, Jessie, landed on his shoulder. "Pieces of eight! Pieces of eight!" she screeched, her bright eyes looking at the gold coins and jewels in the chest.

"That's right, my pretty," said Pirate Pat, taking the wheel from Julian. "And now we'll find a safe place to hide it."

The Flying Postman dropped anchor off a small desert island. The pirates rowed to the shore, leaving Julian the cabin boy on the ship.

Pirate Pat led the way, cutting down trees and bushes with his sharp cutlass. At last, in a clearing, he signalled his men to stop. He handed spades to Sneaky Sam and Awful Alf. "Right, me hearties, start digging!"

While his men dug, Pirate Pat drew a map of the island on a scrap of paper. When it was finished he tucked it into his high boot. "Just so's we know where to come back for the treasure, lads!" he laughed.

The pirates put the treasure chest in the hole they had dug and piled sand and soil on top. "Now that's safe and snug, let's see what else we can nab!" laughed Pirate Pat, and led his men back to the Flying Postman.

That night, as the sun set, Pirate Pat stood on the bridge of his ship, searching the horizon for another treasure ship to attack. Suddenly he put down his spyglass. "There's a big storm brewing, lads," he said. "Take in the sails. Looks like we're in for a rough night."

Dark, boiling clouds rolled towards them across the darkening sky. The sea turned greeny-black, and tall waves started to slap against the sides of the Flying Postman. The ship plunged through the heavy seas, rising up, then plunging down.

Pirate Pat struggled to hold the wheel as the sea boiled up around the ship, heaving and tossing the Flying Postman as if she were a cork.

Rain slashed Pirate Pat's face, sea water swirled around the decks – and the Flying Postman reared up on the huge waves, then fell forward with a sickening lurch.

Pirate Pat could hardly stay on his feet as the ship pitched and rolled, up and down, up and down. Thunder boomed and crashed, and a streak of lightning lit up the black sky.

Suddenly a huge wave, twice as tall as the others, reared up out of the ocean and loomed over the ship. "Look out, lads, look out!" cried Pirate Pat. "It's . . ."

Pat woke with a jolt and looked around. The black sky was replaced by a blue one, and the rolling ship was his hammock, swinging to and fro. "Oh dear," said Pat, and rushed into the house.

Sara looked up as Pat rushed by. Pat looked very green. "What's wrong?" she asked.

Pat didn't stop. "I feel seasick!" he said.

Sara looked at Julian. Julian looked at Sara. "Seasick?" they said together. "Seasick?"

Treasure hunt

Pat was reading a book about pirates. Now he's fallen asleep, and he's dreaming about pirate maps and buried treasure . . .

Play the game with friends. You need a counter each, and a die. Take it in turns to shake the die, moving along the trail through the jungle. The first one to reach the clearing where the treasure is buried is the winner. You must obey the instructions on the trail, and remember – if you land on a square with a gold coin on it, have an **extra throw**. If you land on a square with a pirate flag on it, **miss a turn**.

29

28

27

26

25
Swing on a
creeper. Go
on 1.

24

23
Dead end.
Go back 3.

22

21

20

19

18
Jump a
stream. Go
on 2.

17

finish

40

39

38

16

Run on 3
spaces.

15

14

9

8
Take a short
cut. Go on 2.

10

11

12
Stop to rest.
Miss a turn.

13

7

6

5

Doctor Gilbertson's dance class

Doctor Gilbertson looks after the folk in Greendale when they are ill. But she also likes to keep them fit.

So Doctor Gilbertson runs a women's dance class. "Well done! You are all doing well!" she said.

The men thought the class was very funny. "Dancing around can't make you fit," laughed Ted Glen.

"You would be surprised," replied Doctor Gilbertson. "Dancing is good fun and can make you very fit!"

"Dancing also makes you very bendy, which is most important for fitness," Doctor Gilbertson added.

"We play football to keep us fit," explained Ted. "That is much better than dancing, I'm sure!"

"And during the week we do football training," said Alf. "Lots of press-ups and running on the spot!"

Later that week, it was raining. "The football team won't be able to train today," said Doctor Gilbertson.

Suddenly, the doctor had an idea. She climbed into her car and went to call on Alf Thompson.

She asked Alf if the team would like to join her class. The footballers decided to give it a try.

"This is hard," gasped Ted. "We'll be dancing around the football pitch this time next week!"

Kittens, kittens, kittens

Here are lots of playful kittens. They're black and white, just like Jess. But only two of the kittens are exactly alike. Can you find them?

How many kittens have red collars?
How many kittens have blue collars?
How many kittens are there altogether?

The purrfect pet

Pat, Sara and Julian had just finished breakfast.

"Mum, Dad, can I ask you something?" said Julian.

Pat put down his newspaper. "Of course. What is it?"

"Can I have a new pet?"

Julian's mum and dad looked at one another. "That depends," said Sara. "What sort of pet were you thinking of?"

"I'd really like a dog," said Julian. "A big one, with lots of long hair."

"Looking after a dog is hard work, you know," said Pat. "You'd have to take him for a run three times a day, brush him every day, and . . ."

"Not a dog then," said Julian. "What about a parrot?"

Sara shook her head. "They're very noisy – and I think they're better off in the jungle than in a cage, don't you?"

Julian nodded. "A pony then! That would be fun."

"No," said Pat. "They cost a lot of money – and where would we keep it? Our garden's far too small."

"What about something smaller – stick insects or a goldfish?" Sara suggested.

"Boring," said Julian. "I want something I can talk to and handle – like a snake!"

Pat and Sara looked alarmed.

"A very small snake?" said Julian hopefully.

"No," said Pat.

Sara took out a notepad and pencil. "Let's make a list. Maybe that will give us some ideas."

"Not too big," said Pat.

"Not too small," said Julian.

Sara wrote everything down. "Not too expensive," she added.

"Not too noisy," said Pat.

"A pet that doesn't need a lot of exercise," said Sara.

"And brushing," said Pat.

The list was getting longer and longer.

"A pet you can talk to," said Julian. "And one that's soft and cuddly."

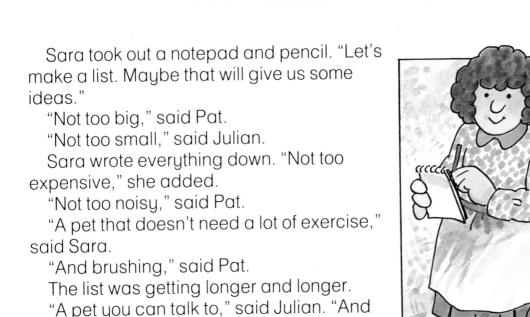

Just then Jess walked in. He jumped up on to Julian's knee. He looked at Julian, blinked, and settled down into a soft round ball.

Pat laughed. "Not too big. Not too small. Not too noisy. Soft and cuddly." He pointed to Jess. "Julian, I think you've already got the **purrfect** pet."

Jess purred softly and went to sleep.

People-spotting

The park looks empty, doesn't it? But it's not – if you look very carefully you'll see bits of people you know. How many can you find and name? Try to find ten.

ICES

DOGS MUST BE ON A LEAD

Strictly for the birds . . .

Julian walked into Forge Cottage and threw his new binoculars down on the table. "It's no good," he said unhappily.

"What's no good?" asked Postman Pat.

"Bird watching," said Julian. "I've been in the woods all morning and I've seen hardly any birds. They seem to know I'm there and fly off."

"You have to be very quiet, you know," said Pat. "Creep up on them."

"I've tried," said Julian. "But they always see me and fly off."

"Come on," said Pat. "Let's try again."

Later, in a quiet clearing in the woods, Pat crouched behind a bush and pointed. "Over there," he whispered. "A woodpecker."

But as he spoke the woodpecker flew away.

Julian looked through his binoculars. "I think there's a wren over there," he said excitedly. "Oh, no, it's flown off into the trees. See, Dad, it's no good – we need to be hidden better."

"Mmmmm," said Pat, thinking hard. "Wait here, Julian, I'll be back in ten minutes."

Pat was soon back, his arms full of streaky, greeny-brown canvas.

"What is it?" asked Julian. "A hide?"

"Not quite," said Pat. "Now just put your head in here . . . and your arms in here . . . and look through these holes."

Seconds later two new 'trees' appeared at the edge of the clearing.

"This is great," said Julian, as a bird flew down and landed on one of his 'branches'.

Pat laughed quietly. "I knew these tree costumes from the Christmas panto would come in useful some time."

Camping out

Sara is putting Julian to bed on a warm summer's evening. "I don't like going to bed when it's daylight," he grumbles.

"And I don't sleep very well because it's too hot to sleep indoors," he says. "Where else can you sleep?" asks Sara.

"I can sleep in my tent outside in the garden," suggests Julian. But Sara doesn't think this is a very good idea.

She tells Pat about it. "Let him sleep in the tent if he wants to," says Pat. "It will be all right, you'll see."

Julian and Pat put the tent up at the bottom of the garden. "Now I don't mind going to bed," says Julian.

Julian snuggles down in his sleeping bag, but he doesn't go to sleep straight away. Soon, it is very dark outside.

Suddenly, a **HOOT!** comes from somewhere in the garden. "Wh-what's that?" he says. He looks outside.

An owl is sitting in a tree. "Was that you?" asks Julian. The owl hoots again and Julian dives back into the tent.

Julian climbs back into his sleeping bag. But just as he is dropping off to sleep, something crawls over his nose!

"What was that?" cries Julian. He switches on his torch to see. "**Phew!** It's only a ladybird!" he says, surprised.

A little while later, Julian hears a loud **CRASH!** outside. But it's only Jess. He's knocked the dustbin lid off!

Julian decides to go back in the house. "Er – I think my bedroom is a better place to sleep, after all," he says.

Jess can hardly believe his ears. What is that terrible noise?

He should have known . . . Pat is singing in the bath again!

Jess rushes downstairs, but Sara is practising on the piano!

Even Julian has funny noises coming out of his ears. Yuk!

Now this is more like it . . . **cat music!** Jess thinks it's great!

Unfortunately, no one else likes it. People are very strange!

Pat's new job

Postman Pat was driving along by the side of Birkmere Lake. He had finished his round early, and was on his way back home.

Suddenly a figure ran into the middle of the road. It was Sam Waldron. He waved his arms around and shouted, "Stop! Stop!"

Pat stopped the van and jumped out. "What's wrong?" he asked. "Has there been an accident?"

"No, but my van's broken down," said Sam. "I'll have to get it towed to the garage. It'll probably be days before I'm back on the road."

"Mmm," said Pat. "Not to worry, I'll give you a lift to the garage."

"Thanks, Pat. But what about my customers? They rely on me, you see. They'll all be waiting for their fruit and vegetables and groceries and things. I can't let them down."

Pat looked at his watch. "Look, I've finished work for the day. Can I help? I could maybe deliver a few . . ."

"Great!" said Sam, and before Pat could finish what he was saying, Sam started to load up Pat's van. Soon the back was full of cardboard boxes and carrier bags filled with fruits, vegetables, tins and bottles.

"Hey, I can't take the whole shop!" said Pat, as Sam piled in another box.

"That's the lot," said Sam. "Sugar for Granny Dryden – she's going to make some jam today. Apples, oranges and bananas for Doctor Gilbertson. Flour and margarine for Miss Hubbard – it's her baking day. Oh – and don't forget these fancy cheeses for Reverend Timms – he ordered them specially for a meeting at the vicarage tonight."

"Sugar, apples, oranges, bananas, flour, margarine, cheeses," Pat repeated.

"Now, Granny Dryden lives at . . ." said Sam, climbing up into the van beside Pat.

"Hey, I know where Granny Dryden lives," said Pat. "I'm a postman, remember?"

Sam laughed. "Of course you are. If **you** don't know where people live, I don't know who does!"

Pat dropped Sam at the garage. "Now you're sure you know who wants what?" asked Sam.

"Of course I am," said Pat. "No problem."

Pat drove to Black Beck Farm first. Granny Dryden was pleased to see Pat. "I've been waiting for this sugar," she said, taking it from Pat's van. She pointed to a big string bag of oranges. "I'll have those too, Pat, then I can make marmalade as well as jam."

Pat's next stop was at Southlands Farm Cottage. Miss Hubbard was working in the garden. "So it is Pat's Mobile Shop today, is it?" she said, when Pat explained about Sam's van. She took her flour and margarine, then saw the basket of cheeses. "Put some cheese on my bill, too, will you, Pat?" she said. "I'll make some cheese flans while the oven's on."

Pat was confused. Cheeses? Weren't they for Granny Dryden – or was it Doctor Gilbertson? But it was too late now – Miss Hubbard (and the cheeses) had gone into the cottage.

Pat sat in the van. "Now where's the next delivery?" he said. "Flour, sugar, margarine, fruit – that's it, fruit for Doctor Gilbertson. Next stop Garner Bridge."

"Apples and bananas – just what the doctor ordered!" joked Pat, handing a carrier bag to Doctor Gilbertson.

"But where are my oranges?" asked Doctor Gilbertson. "I ordered two dozen."

Pat searched the van. "They must be here . . ."

Suddenly he stopped. Oh dear, he'd sold the oranges to Granny Dryden! "I'll come back later with the oranges," said Pat. "All right?"

"Fine," said Doctor Gilbertson. "See you later."

Pat found Reverend Timms outside St Thomas's vicarage. "What was your order, Reverend?" asked Pat.

"Just the cheeses," said Reverend Timms.

Oh no, Pat had sold the cheeses to Miss Hubbard. She was making flans with them! "I've . . . er . . . forgotten the cheeses. I'll bring them later," said Pat, and he drove back to the mobile shop.

By the time Pat had delivered the oranges and cheeses it was five o'clock.

"I'm tired out," Pat told Sara when he got home at last, and he explained that he'd done some deliveries for Sam.

"I bet it made a nice change, didn't it, delivering groceries instead of letters?" said Sara.

"No, it didn't," said Pat. "I'm going to stick to delivering the post in future. And I never want to see a piece of cheese again . . . or an orange."

"That's a pity," said Sara, laughing. "Guess what's for tea? Cheese and potato pie and orange fool!"

Sam's mobile shop

Sara has asked Julian to buy some things from Sam's mobile shop. She wants Julian to buy a cabbage, a cauliflower and a bag of potatoes. How much will the things cost? Julian has a pound to pay for the vegetables. How much change will he take home?

Colour all the things in Sam's shop.

Answer

The vegetables will cost 95p. Julian will get 5p change.

61

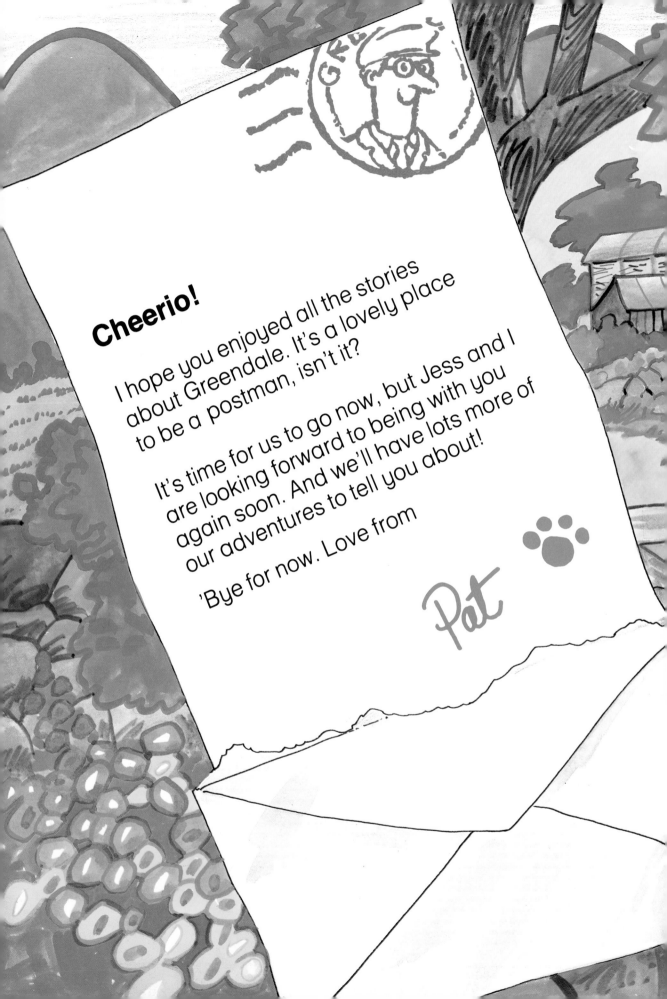

Cheerio!

I hope you enjoyed all the stories about Greendale. It's a lovely place to be a postman, isn't it?

It's time for us to go now, but Jess and I are looking forward to being with you again soon. And we'll have lots more of our adventures to tell you about!

'Bye for now. Love from

Pat